GERONIMO
The Fighting Apache

Ronald Syme

GERONIMO

The Fighting Apache

illustrated by Ben F. Stahl

William Morrow and Company | New York 1975

Library of Congress Cataloging in Publication Data

Syme, Ronald (date)
    Geronimo, the fighting Apache.

    SUMMARY: A biography of the Apache chief who rose to leadership
through the ranks and led one of the last great Indian uprisings in the
nineteenth century.
    1. Geronimo, Apache chief, 1829-1909—Juvenile literature. [1. Ge-
ronimo; Apache chief, 1829-1909. 2. Apache Indians—Biography.
3. Indians of North America—Biography] I. Stahl, Ben F., illus. II. Title.
E99.A6S95   970.3   [B]   [92]   74-16337
ISBN 0-688-22013-4
ISBN 0-688-32013-9 (lib. bdg.)

To Shepard Rifkin, of New York, author and authority on
early America, whose guidance and help have made this
book possible.

APACHE
COUNTRY

Go Khla Yeh

After a summer shower had ceased and the sun was shining again, the land smelled fresh and sweet. The straight rows of corn, the green lines of beans growing in between them, the pumpkins, and the melons gave off a pleasant fragrance.

Caring for those crops was the work of the Apache Indian women, but when Geronimo was a small boy, he loved those sweet-smelling food allotments. Wearing his breechcloth, Go Khla Yeh, as he was called, often scampered among the rows of vegetables where glistening raindrops splashed his bare brown skin. He knew where to find the melon that was ripe and ready for eating or the row of corn where the grain was already golden.

But the Apache people, whose vast territory stretched from central Arizona to northwest Texas, preferred to live by hunting. The planting of fruit and corn and vegetables by their women was merely a pleasant occupation during the summer months. At other times of the year they roamed freely from the Arizona-New Mexico frontier to Texas and northward into Wyoming, hunting deer and buffalo as they went.

The Apache subtribe to which Go Khla Yeh belonged were called the Bedonkohe, and their traditional territory was around the headwaters of the Gila River. Geronimo was born in No-doyohn Canyon, Arizona, in June of the year 1829. During the next ten years, the strength of the Apache nation decreased, even though the people still felt secure in this vast land of sharp-peaked mountains, twisting canyons, fertile valleys, and scorching deserts. It was a country they had inhabited for more than a thousand years, ever since their ancestors had moved southward into it from the Canadian Northwest.

The different climate and environment had affected their nature and culture; they had acquired tribal customs and practices suitable to the country in which they lived. They had become, over the years, a hard, highly intelligent, and physically strong race. Strict discipline, loyalty, fortitude, and endurance were qualities they admired and encouraged. A boy had to be able to hold a mouthful of water and run four miles without spilling or swallowing a drop. At eight or nine years of age Geronimo was learning to hunt both rabbits and turkeys, on foot or from the back of a galloping horse. At twelve he was becoming expert with a bow and spear. By seventeen, if he measured up to the rigid standards, he might proudly assume the rank and dignity of a full-grown warrior.

The girls' training was almost equally strenuous. They were encouraged to become tireless runners. They had to learn to cook, sew, dress hides, swim a river, and climb sheer-sided mountains. There was a reason for this training; in times of war the women and girls sometimes needed to seek safety in flight.

The great annual event for these Apaches was their migration every fall. When the days grew shorter and the weather colder, they departed southward into Mexico for trade. These trips were a wonderful experience for children like Geronimo. They saw unknown birds and animals, ate new fruits, and watched giant butterflies hovering among brightly colored flowers. On their way south their subtribe often met and blended with the Apaches of the Chiricahua subtribe, who were also on their way south. Even the Bedonkohe children knew that the Chiricahua, short, powerful warriors, seldom more than five feet six inches tall, were the fiercest and most warlike people of the Apache nation. The women were sturdy and tireless, and often they could run, fight, and climb almost as well as the men.

"We are the Chihenne, the Red People," the Chiricahua children boasted to their Bedonkohe friends. This name came from the warriors' custom

10

of painting on their faces, for feasts and in time of war, a band of red clay encircling their eyes. By that sign all others knew that they were Chiricahua.

"We are your blood brothers," Geronimo and his friends replied. "The Bedonkohe and the Chiricahua are the bravest fighters of all the Apache nation."

The children were fascinated by everything they saw in Mexico. They stared solemnly at the ponderous Mexican *carretas,* the oxcarts with squealing wooden wheels. They gazed at the white-walled adobe houses in which Mexican families lived. Best of all they enjoyed entering the dark little village stores, where bales of brightly colored cloth and new kerosene lamps were packed beside shining steel knives, coils of rope, hoes, boxes of cartridges, sickles, and strange-looking bottles of wine.

Between the Mexicans and the Apaches there was little liking or trust, even when they were supposed to be at peace. But the Mexicans wanted Indian

blankets and soft, beautifully cured pelts. The Apaches wanted knives, powder, lead, guns, needles, and cloth. They were charged exorbitant prices, but they managed in other ways to reduce the cost of their purchases. Sometimes they raided outlying ranches and helped themselves to horses, which they

drove northward across the border. When Go Khla Yeh was still a boy, the Apaches were beginning to realize the value of slow-moving and obstinate oxen, animals they had formerly despised. Their meat and skins were good items to barter in some town far from the ranch where they had been stolen.

13

After a series of such Apache raids, Mexican cavalry and infantry sometimes appeared. Then came the bad times of shootings and ambushes. Sooner or later the fighting ended, and a distrustful peace returned to the border. Gradually the Apaches went back to their accustomed camping grounds outside the Mexican villages and began to unpack the bales of furs, which the shopkeepers were always eager to buy.

Geronimo's description of those trips appears in the story of his life related in his own words by an Oklahoman named S. H. Barrett. In it Geronimo says:

We usually stayed for several days, camping outside those villages. Every day our people would go into the town to trade. They always left our camp under a small guard so that our arms, supplies, and women and children would not be disturbed during our absence.

14

The Mexicans never worried the Apaches greatly, even though Mexican bounty hunters sometimes came as far north as the Gila River in search of Indian scalps. They were paid at the rate of $100 for a warrior's scalp and $50 for a woman's. But those detested killers were few and far between. They knew what would happen to them if they were caught by the Apaches. Scalping, a practice originated by the early white settlers in North America, was particularly detested by Geronimo's tribe.

The Apaches knew vaguely of the white race far to the east of them. They called those people the White Eyes. Up to Geronimo's youth, however, the only White Eyes the Apaches had seen were small and threadbare exploring parties and wandering prospectors. The Indians were inclined to be friendly with these rather futile strangers. They had no idea then of the great and imminent threat to their people that was already looming on the horizon. Unknown to the 30,000 Apaches, important

White Eyes appear
in Apache country

events were taking place between the United States Government and the Government of Mexico.

In 1848, when Geronimo was nineteen years old, Mexico ceded to the United States, by the Treaty of Guadalupe Hidalgo, nearly all the territory in the present states of California, Nevada, Utah, Colorado, Arizona, and New Mexico. In that same year gold was discovered in California. Across the silent plains, arroyos, and deserts of Apache country, lumbering ox-drawn wagons, escorted by armed outriders, began to appear. The first fortified cabins of lonely pioneers were soon being built.

The more northerly Apaches, resentful but less warlike than their southern blood brothers, raided a few caravans and killed occasional small parties of the White Eyes. But they made no concerted effort to wipe out these strangers whom they despised for their crazy lust for gold, a metal the Indians regarded as worthless.

The Chiricahua warriors of New Mexico were

17

more hostile. Before long they were recognized by the United States authorities as a dangerous obstacle to white settlement of the Territory. Geronimo's own tribe was beginning to side with the Chiricahua, who at that time were led by their great chief, Cochise.

Geronimo, now twenty-nine years old, was one of those who set out southward in 1858 on the customary trek into Mexico. It was the last time he would ever make that journey with thoughts of peace in his mind. With him were his widowed mother, his young wife, Alope, and their three small children. Hostilities with the Mexicans had ceased, and no unusual danger was to be expected south of the border. The Apaches entered Sonora openly and without taking many precautions. On reaching the outskirts of a small town they called Kas-ki-yeh, they pitched camp. The women and children were left in the care of the usual small guard. The rest of

the warriors went into the village to trade their furs
and blankets. In the words of Geronimo's life story:

> Late that afternoon when returning from
> town we were met by a few women and
> children who told us that Mexican troops from
> some other town had attacked our camp, killed
> all the warriors of the guard, captured all our
> ponies, secured our arms, destroyed our sup-
> plies, and killed many of our women and
> children.

The Bedonkohe scattered into the rocky hills and
bush-choked ravines until darkness. Cautiously they
then crept back to their destroyed camp. Geronimo's story continues:

> I found that my aged mother, my young
> wife, and my three small children were among
> the slain. There were only eighty warriors left,

and as we were without arms or supplies, and were furthermore surrounded by the Mexicans far inside their territory, we could not hope to fight successfully. So our chief, Mangus-Colorado, gave the orders to start at once in perfect silence for our homes in Arizona, leaving the dead upon the field.

The shock of that senseless massacre affected Geronimo for the rest of his life. Until that time there had been nothing outstanding about his prowess or achievements as a warrior. But from then on Geronimo changed. A hard-faced, broad-shouldered warrior with implacable eyes and a thin-lipped, ruthless mouth, he soon sought revenge. Eagerly he took part in meetings between the Bedonkohe, the Nedni Apaches under their giant chief, Juh, and the red-banded Chiricahua.

In the summer of 1859, nearly a year after the massacre, the warriors of these three subtribes rode southward to the Mexican border. They wore their war paint and the war bands, strips of deerskin about two inches wide fastened round their heads. All of them carried firearms, mostly either Sharps rifles or Hall carbines. By barter, violence, or theft, the Apaches never had any great difficulty in obtaining guns, although ammunition supplies were sometimes hard to come by.

The Mexican troopers responsible for the murder of the Apache women and children came from Nacozari, a town 100 miles south of the border. On its outskirts the Apaches captured and killed eight Mexican civilians. Geronimo recalled:

This was to draw the troops from the city, and the next day they came. Just at night we captured their supply train, so we had plenty of provisions and some more guns.

About ten o'clock in the morning the whole Mexican force came out. There were two com-

panies of cavalry and two of infantry. I recognized the cavalry as the soldiers who had killed my people at Kas-ki-yeh. This I told to the chieftains [Cochise, Juh, and Mangus-Colorado] and they said that I might direct the battle.

The Apaches remained hidden in the undergrowth of a belt of forest until the Mexicans came within 100 yards of the nearest trees. At that moment they rose to their feet, discharged a single volley, dropped their rifles, and charged with spears and tomahawks.

The battle lasted two hours. The ill-trained and inexperienced Mexican infantry were no match for warriors accustomed to warfare since boyhood. The cavalry, encircled by infantry and Apaches, were unable to reform. The Mexican force was completely wiped out.

Geronimo says:

Over the bloody field, covered with the bodies of Mexicans, rang the fierce Apache war whoop. Still covered with the blood of my enemies, I was surrounded by the Apache braves and made war chief of all the Apaches. . . . The Apaches had revenged the massacre of Kas-ki-yeh.

At this battle, the Mexicans called Go Khla Yeh, Geronimo, the name by which he has been known ever since. From then on, and until the end of his fighting days, he was the most wanted Apache in Mexico. Mexican troops planned one ambush after another for him. Frequently they made hasty and hopeless attacks on entrenched war parties of Apaches as soon as they discovered that Geronimo was one of the band. But he was never taken prisoner, either by Americans or Mexicans, nor was he ever forced to surrender.

In their own territory to the north the Apaches

Geronimo 1859

were at last growing aware of the menace of advancing civilization. Fights and skirmishes, attacks on the Overland Mail, and murders and outrages on both sides became sadly frequent. Modern American historians, more liberal in their outlook than those of earlier times, admit frankly that the white settlers and soldiers were more callous and even more treacherous than their Apache enemies.

Soldiers stationed at Fort Whipple near Prescott in western Arizona shot all Apaches — men, women and children — whom they came across. A group of white settlers, allegedly with some Army officers among them, invited a party of Apache warriors to a supposed peace conference and then fed the Indians poisoned piñole nuts. An effort was made at an Army camp to arrest the chief, Cochise, when he appeared with a white flag on a peaceful mission. Cochise managed a daring escape by slitting the wall of a tent with his hunting knife. The five subchiefs who had accompanied him were hanged.

It was a black period of history for both the white men and the Indians. The list of wrongs was lengthy, and it continued to increase during the late 1850's and early 1860's, especially after gold was discovered in Arizona. The United States Government did not improve matters by declaring its determination to "exterminate the Apache as quickly as possible."

Geronimo and his tribe were no longer safe from attack anywhere in their own territory. The summer fruit and vegetable allotments were abandoned. Hunting for food and clothing became increasingly dangerous; indeed, the Apaches were being gradually forced to live like wild animals. Parties of white soldiers, bands of armed civilians, and bounty killers roamed the countryside, watching for the enemy at water springs, beside traditional Indian trails, and in fertile valleys. Such an existence was hard enough on the warriors; it was cruel and almost unbearable for the women and children.

The northern and western Apaches reluctantly resigned themselves to surrender and submission. But the Chiricahua and their closest kinsmen, the Bedonkohe, refused to yield. So fiercely and daringly did they strike back at the White Eyes that for a few years it seemed possible that the settlers might have to abandon central Arizona. By secret trails known only to themselves, the southern Apaches continued to avoid capture. They found reasonable safety in their own beloved Chiricahua Mountains or by moving southward into Sonora's Sierra Madre range, where among towering peaks 8000 to 10,000 feet in altitude they knew of hidden fertile valleys.

The United States Government finally decided to build a number of forts throughout New Mexico and Arizona. Among them were Camp Goodwin on the Gila River and Fort Apache on the White River near the eastern frontier of Arizona. But by 1870, the Government irritably realized that the Territory of Arizona lacked the military strength and organization to wipe out the Apaches. Cavalry could not exist in the desert and were totally unfamiliar with local conditions. Slow-moving infantry, accompanied by supply wagons, could never overtake the swifter Indians. Even more humiliating was the fact that in one encounter after another the Apaches proved their ability to fight as well as trained soldiers and to shoot with much more accuracy.

It was a desperate period. In the Fort Grant massacre of 1871, a large party of armed civilians from nearby Tucson murdered, with knives and clubs, seventy-five western Apache women and children who were lying asleep in their huts. This crime occurred during a time when those Apaches had made peace with the United States Government and were presumably under the protection of the military. (In the subsequent trial, all the murderers were found not guilty.)

Shaken by such events, the Government decided

on a peace policy for Arizona. All the Apaches were to be settled on their own lands, which would be theirs forever — so they were told. In addition, they would be protected against hostile whites and encouraged to develop their own agriculture and to raise livestock.

One of these reservations consisted of a large tract of land around Fort Apache in eastern Arizona between the Little Colorado River and the Salt River. Another was at Camp Verde on the Mogollon Mesa. It was located on the Verde River, some distance south of the modern town of Flagstaff. A third reservation was at Camp Grant, in central Arizona. In New Mexico, a large, fertile, and well-watered reservation was set aside at Ojo Caliente (Warm Springs) for the Chiricahua and their kinsmen subtribes. In this area were heavy forests of oak and cottonwood containing deer, elk, turkey, and bear.

These reservations were the only humane plan so far devised by the Government. Seeing that the

Apaches had no chance whatsoever of being able to resist indefinitely the westward march of civilization, the next best thing was to place them in pleasant and fertile areas where they would be strictly protected by law and supervised by capable and understanding officials. But the whole scheme was thrown together in a hurry and badly supervised. The wrong kind of officials were often selected. Politicians took no active interest in the creation of the reservations. The Apaches continued to endure indignities, mishandling, and lying swindles. Sometimes even worse things happened to them.

Geronimo later recalled:

Mangus-Colorado [chief of the Warm Springs Apaches] and about half of our [Chiricahua] people went to New Mexico, happy that now they had found white men who would be kind to them, and with whom they could live in peace and plenty.

32

No word ever came from them. From other sources, however, we heard that they had been treacherously captured and slain.

This was a somewhat inaccurate statement. Although a number of the Chiricahua who went with Mangus-Colorado, a splendid old fighting chief,

Mangus-Colorado

may have been killed later, it seems that the chief himself was the only one who was deliberately murdered. His death occurred in a United States military camp at Mesilla on the Rio Bravo. There Mangus-Colorado surrendered voluntarily, and as he did so he uttered to his friends the prophetic words, "This is my end. I shall never again hunt over the mountains and through the valleys of my people."

His premonition of death was accurate. That night he was shot dead while he lay asleep.

Fierce, surly, and suspicious, Geronimo remained at large, like a wild cat in its native haunts. He knew that his existence was becoming more precarious every day. General George Crook had assumed formal command of United States military forces in Arizona during 1871. He was a thoughtful, capable, and kindly officer, who believed that the Apaches were not being treated fairly. In spite of his sympathy for them, however, he became the best Indian fighter the Army ever produced. The troops under

34

General
George Crook

him swiftly and bloodily smashed the Tonto
Apaches, who lived on the western frontier of
Arizona and in eastern California. After the death
of hundreds of their warriors, the survivors, accompanied by their women and children, were led into
semicaptivity on the notorious San Carlos reservation in the arid, sweltering, and barren country of
the Gila River. Crook then turned his attention to
the still defiant little subtribes of Bedonkohe and
Chiricahua Apaches.

Geronimo and his people found a temporary sanctuary in the fertile range they loved so well. It lay in the Chiricahua Mountains, running southward from Apache Pass in Arizona across the border into Mexico. With Crook now opposed to him, however, even this lonely eyrie became threatened. Crook, ambling through the passes on his old mule, Apache, seemed to have a strange intuition that guided him to the Indians' lairs. Geronimo had one narrow escape after another from capture or death. He said in his life story:

We were surprised and attacked by United States troops, who killed in all seven Indians — one warrior, three women, and three children. The Government troops were mounted and so were we, but we were poorly armed [they had loaned their rifles to the unfortunate Tontos], so we fought mainly with spears, bows, and arrows. Once I was surrounded, but by dodging from side to side of my horse as he ran, I escaped. During this fight we scattered in all directions and two days later reassembled about fifty miles from the scene of this battle.

About ten days later the same United States troops attacked our new camp at sunrise. The fight lasted all day, but our arrows and spears were all gone before ten o'clock, and for the remainder of the day we had only rocks and clubs with which to fight. We could do little damage with these weapons, and at night we moved our camp about four miles back into the mountains where it would be hard for the cavalry to follow us.

Hunted unceasingly from hilltop to hilltop, the Chiricahua had little leisure in which to replenish their stocks of food, clothing, and weapons. Increasingly they were being left to fight the White Eyes alone. The great chief, Cochise, died in 1874. Victorio, the new chief of the Warm Springs Apaches, was living quietly with his people at Ojo Caliente, hoping that — as rumor said — this splendid reservation was not going to be taken away from them. The Tonto Apaches had been smashed and destroyed; they would never fight again.

Early in 1879, fifty-year-old Geronimo with his tattered, ill-armed warriors and their exhausted, threadbare women and children finally decided in favor of peace.

He later said:

When I went to Apache Pass (Fort Bowie), I found a General Howard in command, and made a treaty with him. This treaty lasted until long after General Howard had left our country. He always kept his word with us and treated us as brothers. We could have lived forever at peace with him. After he went away he placed an agent at Apache Pass who issued to us from the Government clothing, rations, and supplies.

If the political leaders in Washington had been humane and possessed any integrity, Arizona and the neighboring states might have forgotten the name of Geronimo. But because those politicians were corrupt and greedy, this relatively peaceful time proved to be only temporary.

Throughout 1879, Geronimo and his 300 to 400

1877-1881
President
Hayes

Chiricahua lived in the comparative freedom of their own mountains. Game of all kinds was plentiful, and none of the White Eyes interfered with them. And then the blow fell.

The news came from Washington. The Warm Springs reservation and the Chiricahua reservation were to be taken away from the Apache nation. No compensation was to be paid for this confiscation of land, which had been given to the Indians with the solemn promise that it would remain theirs "for as long as the mountains shall stand." As of today it has still not been returned to the Apache people.

Worst of all, however, was the news that from then on all Apaches were to be taken to the San Carlos reservation. There they were to be herded together and abandoned to a miserable, aimless existence with scanty rations, inadequate clothing and blankets, no medical supervision, and little hope of being able to provide extra food for themselves.

The prospect was too much for Geronimo and his

undying, brooding hatred of all the White Eyes. Instead, as he later described, he went off on his own:

> We separated, each leader taking his own band. Some of them went to San Carlos and some to Old Mexico, but I took my own people back to Warm Springs and rejoined Victorio's band.

Victorio knew that the Government had decided to seize the Warm Springs reservation. But the area had always belonged to his tribe, and they loved it greatly. The land was rich and fertile, the surrounding hills and forests and mountains were plentiful with game. The Warm Springs Indians with Victorio were still hoping that by some miracle they would be overlooked by the soldiers. They were living peacefully and interfering with no one in the hope of avoiding official attention. In order to remain in their favorite area, they were prepared to run the risk of being shot on sight by soldiers or armed civilians, the penalty decreed by the Government for any Indians found off a reservation. They preferred their present way of life to that of some of the Chiricahua who, under Taza and Naiche (Natchez), the sons of Cochise, had plodded off to San Carlos.

Naiche

General Crook was still sympathetic toward the Apaches, but he had his orders to fulfill. The last of the tribe must be rounded up. His men appeared at the Warm Springs reservation, and Geronimo surrendered voluntarily to them. He described the scene later in these words:

Two companies of [Indian] scouts were sent from San Carlos. When they came to Warm Springs they sent word for me and Victorio to come to town. As soon as we arrived, soldiers met us, disarmed us, and took us both to headquarters. Victorio was released and I was sentenced to the guardhouse and put in chains. When I asked them why they did this, they said it was because I had left Apache Pass.

I do not think that I ever belonged to those soldiers at Apache Pass, or that I should have asked them where I might go.

I was kept prisoner for four months, during which time I was transferred to San Carlos. Then I think I had another trial, although I

Geronimo
in chains

was not present. In fact, I do not know that I had another trial, but I was told that I had, and at any rate, I was released.

If the American authorities had deliberately tried to make Geronimo an even more dangerous enemy, they could scarcely have done better. He was a warrior and proud of his standing in the tribe. To be loaded into a mule cart and taken in chains to San Carlos, where many hundreds of Apaches saw his humiliation, was a terrible disgrace. To be confined for months in a small prison cell under constant guard was a terrible punishment to a man like Geronimo to whom freedom was part of his natural heritage.

Victorio and 400 of his followers had also been brought under armed guard to San Carlos. There were now more than 5000 silent, moody, and depressed Apaches — men, women and children — living on that dreary reservation.

They were in a mood of bitter resentment. The President had sent them word through his official representatives that under their chief, Victorio, they would be free to remain permanently within their territory at Ojo Caliente. Yet only two years after that promise had been made, they were removed by armed soldiers and brought to the reservation at San Carlos. They told each other bitterly that perhaps the reason was that White Eyes might have suspected the presence of gold in the surrounding mountains. Gold, declared the Apaches, apparently counted for more than the solemn word of the Great White Chief, who had ordered them to be brought to the worst place in all Apache country.

Camp Goodwin on the Gila River was the local headquarters for these Indians. Built as a cavalry barracks in 1864, it had been abandoned within a few years owing to the dangerous prevalence of malaria fever, carried by mosquitoes that bred in the nearby swamps.

Much of Arizona had a reasonably temperate climate, but in the level, sandy country around Camp Goodwin the heat was intolerable. United States politicians expected the wretched Apaches to inhabit this area rather than to seek relief in the higher surrounding country, even though they would still be within the limits of the reservation. It was a harsh restriction on the tribe.

Lieutenant Britton Davis, a twenty-two-year-old Texan, arrived to undertake military duties at Camp

Lieutenant
Britton Davis

Goodwin in 1882. He was a fair-minded young officer, the son of a judge. Before long the Apaches recognized him as possessing the qualities that they themselves most admired — honesty, courage, and justice. During the next four years, Davis came to understand and respect the Apache Indians. Long years after he resigned his commission in 1886, he wrote an excellent book about Geronimo and this period of Arizona history. To this day, *The Truth About Geronimo* remains a most valuable reference work.

Of the site chosen by the Government as suitable territory for the Apache Indians, Davis wrote:

A gravelly flat, it was dotted here and there by the drab adobe buildings of the Agency. Scrawny, dejected lines of scattered cottonwoods, shrunken, almost lifeless, marked the course of the streams. Rain was so infrequent that it seemed like a phenomenon

48

when it came at all. Almost continuously dry, hot, dust- and gravel-laden winds swept the plain, denuding it of every vestige of vegetation. In summer a temperature of 110 degrees in the shade was cool weather. At all other times of the year flies, gnats, unnameable bugs swarmed in millions. Everywhere the naked, hungry, dirty, frightened little Indian children, darting behind bushes or into wikiups [low, crudely thatched huts] at sight of you. Everywhere the sullen, stolid, hopeless, suspicious faces of the older Indians challenging you. San Carlos was our idea of 'Hell's Forty Acres.'

Davis might have added that conditions on the reservation were sometimes made worse by the often dishonest or apathetic Indian Agents who came and went. Those obscure officials were assisted in their authority and duties by a number of white

San Carlos reservation

scouts, most of whom were hard-faced gunslingers with no time for any live Indian. They saw no reason why the Apaches should be treated as human beings and seldom troubled to do so themselves.

The Government had devised a number of hazy ideas about encouraging the Apaches to take up agriculture. But during the early days on the San Carlos reservation, the lack of irrigation, tools, and seeds made the scheme impossible. Not even a promised herd of cattle appeared. The Apaches refused to raise hogs, an animal they despised because it ate snakes. Day after day the Indians were left idle, ill-fed, and with nothing to occupy their minds or bodies.

Geronimo was one of the worst affected by this miserable existence. His naturally surly and suspicious nature heightened his resentment and hatred. He became morose, ill-tempered, and, according to Davis, began to drink too much of the tiswin beer, which the Indian women brewed from corn. Before long he earned a reputation among the white officials as a deceitful man whose word was not to be trusted. Geronimo held the same views regarding the White Eyes. The wretched existence his people were leading at San Carlos was final proof to him that no white Americans could ever be trusted.

Victorio and Geronimo abandoned the reservation in the fall of 1881. With them went 310 followers — men, women, and children. Among them was the great young woman warrior, Lozen. She was so honored and respected by the men that they granted her a place in their tribal councils. Juh and his son, Delshinne, and a splendid old veteran chief named Nana also rode with the fugitives. How Geronimo's band procured rifles and horses remains a mystery. They were, however, well armed and well mounted.

News of the outbreak reached the camp police while the party was still moving out. Police Chief Sterling rode after them and ordered the Apaches to return. When they refused to do so, he swung up his rifle to shoot the subchief, Loco. Another Indian, moving more swiftly, shot Sterling dead.

While frantically clicking telegraph keys warned settlements throughout the southwest, Geronimo, Juh, and the other leaders guided their people along Indian trails that led south. Geronimo says:

We went on toward Old Mexico, but on the second day after this United States soldiers [cavalry] overtook us about three o'clock in the afternoon and we fought until dark. The ground where we were attacked was very rough, which was to our advantage, for the troops were compelled to dismount in order to fight us. I do not know how many soldiers were killed, but we lost only one warrior and three children. We had plenty of guns and ammunition we had accumulated while living on the reservation and the remainder we had obtained from the White Mountain Apaches when we left the reservation.

Another Apache, a young boy named Kaywaykla who took part in this flight, lived until 1963. In later years he published an account of his tragic experiences. He wrote of this incident, in which three soldiers died:

> They spent two nights at that place. Ussen [the Apache God] had delivered them from bondage and they were obligated to render thanks to Him according to their custom — with song and dance. Once in the mountains they could rest and rejoice, a free people again. In the land of Juh [a spacious and fertile sanctuary high up in the Sierra Madre] there would be no pursuit. Security and abundance would come in a short time. The horrors of San Carlos would fade.

Almost as soon as they reached the border they were located and attacked again, this time by Mexican cavalry. Once more those heroic Apaches, men and women alike, beat off one attack after another with accurate rifle fire. The older boys joined in whenever they could find a spare rifle, even though the recoil of a heavy Springfield bruised their shoulders and sometimes knocked them down.

Kaywaykla wrote:

Lozen, her head concealed by a screen of cactus, dropped a man with every shot. Three times the Mexicans charged before deciding that the Apaches were not to be dislodged by that means.

Skirmishing and fighting almost every day, the Apaches finally reached comparative safety in the mountains.

The Sierra Madre range rose in places to a height

of 12,000 feet. On its western side, in the state of Sonora, the mountains resembled a giant comb, high ridges of rock forming the teeth. Between them were deep valleys, usually choked with undergrowth. From high in these sierras the Apaches were able to descend by secret paths to obtain necessary supplies from nearby Mexican villages. Pursuing troops were unable to follow them into the mountains.

Juh, in spite of his great size and formidable prowess as a warrior, had a more amiable nature than Geronimo. During an earlier stay in the Sierra Madre, he had established a reasonably friendly relationship with the Mexicans of the settlements. He used it to trade with them now. Probably there was not much honesty on either side. If the Apaches stole a herd of cattle or horses in Sonora, they took the animals through the passes and sold them in Chihuahua, the state that lay east of the mountains. At other times they reversed the process. The Mex-

Lozen

ican traders drove hard bargains, but they were happy to exchange rifles, ammunition, clothing, needles, knives, and a potent spirit called mescal for animals that they were buying very cheaply. They were not able to rely on their own troops for protection, so they preferred to remain on more or less friendly terms with the Apaches.

In Arizona, a first-class political row built up as a result of the Apaches' flight. The settlers in lonely areas were alarmed and outraged. Officials began to take a closer look at the San Carlos reservation. What they discovered was too much even for their smug consciences.

In October, 1882, a Federal grand jury charged that Agent Tiffany of San Carlos "had kept eleven men in confinement for fourteen months without charges or any attempt to accuse them, knowing them to be innocent."

The shocking indictment of reservation conditions continued:

The present investigations of the grand jury have laid bare the infamy of Agent Tiffany and a proper idea can be formed of the fraud and villainy which are constantly practised in open violation of the law and in defiance of public justice. Frauds, speculation, conspiracy, larceny, plots, and counterplots seem to be the rule of action upon the reservation.

Agent Tiffany was properly punished, but his imprisonment did not bring Geronimo and his Apaches back to the reservation. San Carlos was hastily improved. Army officers, who were almost always more fair-minded than civilian agents, were given powers to run the place, and large-scale military operations were begun to recapture the missing Apaches. Indian scouts, who were invaluable to the troops in their knowledge of Apache ways, were persuaded or bribed into recruitment.

Unfortunately, the reformation of San Carlos did

not include the swift dismissal of some of the white scouts. Men such as Al Sieber and Micky Free should

Micky Free

never have been given authority over any Indians anywhere in the United States.

Sieber, a 190-pound Pennsylvania Dutchman, was undoubtedly an efficient chief scout. He was also a natural gunman and utterly ruthless toward all Indians. On one occasion he was known to have gunned down an Apache prisoner in order to economize on the rations. He was detested and feared by the Indians, one of whom in later years shot and crippled him for life.

Micky Free was the son of a Mexican mother and a drunken Irish father. He had been raised by the Apaches after he had taken refuge as a boy in one of their camps. As an interpreter he was never to be trusted. The Indians grew to detest Free, and even Sieber could not tolerate the fellow.

Most of the large band of Indian scouts were brave and reliable men who, in exchange for eight dollars a month, the possession of a rifle, and a distinguishing red headband, had agreed to help the White Eyes. But two of them, Chato and Tzoe, were bad characters who were hated by their own people.

Chato had been a promising young warrior, who had fought with the Warm Springs Apaches against the military. For some unknown reason he had gone over to the White Eyes. Since then he had opposed his own people.

Chato

Tzoe (nicknamed Peaches by the soldiers because of his light complexion) was another young and stalwart warrior. He had deserted Juh's stronghold in the Sierra Madre and hastily volunteered as a scout. His nickname among the Apaches was Yellow Wolf. "In contempt for his treachery," said Kaywaykla.

With such men as Sieber, Free, Chato, and Tzoe acting as go-betweens, there could be no hope of a satisfactory relationship with the Apaches.

Tzoe (Peaches)

Still, General Crook sent some of his best Indian scouts into Sonora to make contact with the fugitive Apaches. As the Mexican authorities were anxious to see the last of Geronimo and his warriors, they gave official permission for United States troops to cross the border into Mexico. Crook was able to move southward and meet the Indians nearer to their refuge in the mountains. Shortly before his arrival, the Apaches suffered a great loss when their beloved chief, Juh, was accidentally drowned while crossing a stream. Victorio had been killed earlier in a Mexican ambush at Tres Castillos. Geronimo found himself almost alone in his determination never to return to San Carlos. The approach of winter was beginning to weaken the convictions of the rest of the party. Game would be scarce, and without proper food or shelter life would be almost insupportable during the coming months of snow and falling temperatures. Crook arrived at the right time.

To the American camp in northeast Sonora came Geronimo, Naiche, and other Apache leaders.

Crook treated them with courteous honesty. He told them about the improvements he had ordered at San Carlos. There would be no more swindling of rations and no more crooked civilian administrators. No longer would the Chiricahua Apaches have to live near Camp Goodwin and report every day for roll call.

Kaywaykla wrote:

Lieutenant Britton Davis promised that if we came in we would be permitted to live on Turkey Creek not far from Fort Apache. *Enjuh*! (Good). That country was to our liking — mountainous, with streams, timber, game, and privacy.

Fifty-three-year-old Geronimo had learned enough about the world of the White Eyes to know that wealth was essential in it. If he was going to live on any reservation, then he was going to do so in style. When he and his 300 followers arrived at the border, where Davis and the soldiers awaited him, he came with 350 head of stolen Mexican cattle!

"The Mexicans have given Americans the right to enter their country," protested Davis. "Likewise we have given Mexican soldiers the right to enter ours. Now you want to rest here for three days, Geronimo, in order to refresh those cattle. What will happen if the Mexicans follow you?"

"Mexicans!" growled Geronimo. "My squaws can whip all the Mexicans in Chihuahua."

"But the Mexicans have plenty of cartridges and you have practically none," said Davis.

"We don't fight the Mexicans with cartridges," Geronimo replied haughtily. "Cartridges cost too much. We fight Mexicans with rocks."

Geronimo took his cattle into Arizona, but the animals were not given the rest they needed. The band went on north later that night, and Davis was left to argue matters with the United States Marshal for southern Arizona and the Collector of Customs from Nogales, the Arizona port of entry from Mexico. Both these officials wanted to take Geronimo and his warriors to Tucson to stand trial on a charge of smuggling cattle into the United States.

Geronimo finally lost his cattle. They were taken from him when he reached San Carlos on his way to Turkey Creek. The beef was used for the reservation, the United States Government compensated the

Mexican owners, and Geronimo himself never collected a cent. The incident was another blow to his pride, another reason for his unceasing hatred of the White Eyes.

The Chiricahua, along with some of their tribe from San Carlos, took up residence in the cooler climate and pleasant surroundings of Turkey Creek on the rim of the Mogollon Mesa. Life became more pleasant for them. Besides being a beauty spot, Turkey Creek was rich in game. Deer and bear roamed the forest in great numbers. The 550 Chiricahua began to settle down peacefully under the firm but honest administration of Lieutenant Davis, the only white officer at Turkey Creek. With him were 50 Indian scouts, including the interpreter Micky Free and Al Sieber. Those two hoodlums soon ruined everything.

Geronimo says:

Had the money spent for plows, wagons,

and implements, whose use we did not understand, been put into cattle, we might have been ready to remain at Turkey Creek. But we received those useless things which somebody in Washington thought were the best for us.

Lieutenant Thomas Cruse, later a brigadier general, knew the Apaches and sympathized with them. "These Indians are not agriculturists," he declared. "They are men who from the dawn of history have ranged constantly over the rugged country, killing their food. To them freedom is life."

The Apaches, even the embittered Geronimo, tried to adjust themselves to their new and restricted existence. Some of them made earnest and occasionally successful efforts to plant the soil with strange new crops.

High on a shady ridge, apart from the other Indian huts, Geronimo built a lonely cabin for himself. With Davis he was reserved but polite. For the

Indian scouts he showed no respect or patience. Micky Free in particular he despised and hated. In this fact lay the roots of fresh trouble. Free, Sieber, Chato, and Tzoe seem to have been determined to annoy Geronimo in every way they could. According to Geronimo himself, Free told him that General Crook was planning to have him flung into prison.

One night Micky Free and Chato crept into Davis's tent and told him that a Chiricahua Apache named Kaytennae and Geronimo were planning a mutiny. An older and entirely honest Chiricahua scout named Chihuahua both saw and heard the two rascals. According to Kaywaykla, this is what happened next:

The next morning Chihuahua presented himself to Lieutenant Davis. Micky Free offered to interpret, and Chihuahua ordered him to close his mouth with its forked tongue. He called for Sam Bowman [a Choctaw Indian scout whom the Apaches regarded as honest]. "I have served as scout much longer than Chato," said Chihuahua. "I have served faithfully and told no lies. I have not sneaked to your tent at night. But I am not a spy, and I will not work for anyone who employs one."

Chihuahua removed his military equipment, the red headband worn by all scouts, ammunition belt, and shirt. He placed them in a heap in the corner. "Take this stuff and give it to your spies," he said, and walked angrily out of the tent.

The arrest of Kaytennae without fair proof was one of the few mistakes, and certainly the worst, that Britton Davis made during his period of duty among the Apaches. The unlucky Kaytennae was sentenced without a proper trial to five years' imprisonment at Alcatraz in San Francisco Bay. When he was released, he was completely broken in spirit.

Geronimo had not been planning an escape. Nor had any of the other Apache leaders. But Micky Free, sneaking and whispering around the camp like the paid informer he was, continued to spread malicious rumors about the fate that would soon overtake Geronimo and other leading Apaches.

Geronimo said:

We held a council and, fearing treachery, decided to leave the reservation. We thought it more manly to die on the warpath than to be killed in prison.

On May 17, 1885, about 140 Indians, of whom 41 were warriors, left the reservation. Nana, the great old veteran, was among them, even though he was now well into his seventies. So were Daklugie, the son of Juh, and Istee, the son of Victorio. Chihuahua, the honorable Indian ex-scout, volunteered to lead one small party comprised mostly of women and boys. Before leaving the reservation, the Apaches cut the telegraph wires and hid the severed ends so that the breaks would be difficult to trace.

Chihuahua's party had the misfortune to be ambushed by pursuing cavalry. Most of its members managed to escape on their horses, but a woman who was shot through the leg and a boy with a wounded arm were among the prisoners. They were all taken under escort to Fort Bowie, where the women were set to work digging a ditch.

Kaywaykla wrote:

The crippled woman struggled to work with the rest. She fell down and a soldier beat her with his rifle until she never got up again. Next morning her body was gone.

The Indians never discovered what happened to those unfortunate prisoners. All they could say was that none of them were ever seen again. Once again the White Eyes had shown how cruel they could be.

Geronimo later described what happened to his group:

> After this battle, we rode south of Casas Grandes and made camp, but within a few days this camp was attacked by Mexican soldiers. We skirmished with them all day, killing a few Mexicans but sustaining no loss ourselves. That night we went east into the foothills of the Sierra Madre Mountains and made another camp. We reckoned that about 2000 soldiers were ranging these mountains and seeking to capture us.

Among those troops was Lieutenant Davis with 130 Indian scouts and a 40-man troop of cavalry. From all over Arizona and New Mexico, more troops joined in the search. But 37 Apache warriors, han-

dicapped by the presence of 90 women and children, continued to outwit the searchers.

General Crook quickly realized that ordinary troops were of no use in the lonely mountains. He sent two columns of Apache scouts into the sierras under the command of Lieutenant Davis and three other experienced young officers.

The scouts moved endlessly across the flanks of the mountains. They endured terrific heat, shortage of rations, fever, and the constant danger of an ambush. The tracking skill of the scouts enabled them to follow Geronimo's trail, but they never managed to surprise the wily old leader. However, the fugitive Apaches were soon facing their old problem: lack of food, ammunition, and clothing.

The scouts finally gave up the search. They had to, for Indians and officers alike were in a state of utter exhaustion. In September, 1885, four months after Geronimo had deserted Turkey Creek, Davis and his scouts reached El Paso in Texas.

Davis wrote:

I was ragged and dirty, wearing a four months' beard, an old pair of black trousers partially repaired with white thread. My shoes had rawhide soles and my hair was sticking through holes in my campaign hat.

In the Sierra Madre Geronimo's party still held on to their precarious liberty. Davis's account continues:

They did so for eight months in a country measuring 200 miles by 400 miles. Against them were 500 troops, 500 Indian scouts and irregulars, and every American or Mexican settler with a gun.

In January, 1886, General Crook established contact through his scouts with Geronimo. The site was

78

a pleasantly wooded valley only twelve miles south of the border.

Geronimo describes the meeting in these words:

When I arrived, General Crook said to me, "Why did you leave the reservation?" I said: "You told me that I might live in the reservation the same as white people lived. One year I raised a crop of corn, and gathered and stored it, and the next year I put in a crop of oats, and when the crop was almost ready to harvest, you told your soldiers to put me in prison, and if I resisted to kill me."

General Crook said: "I never gave any such orders. The troops who spread this report knew that it was untrue." Then I agreed to go back with him to San Carlos.

During the long meeting between Crook and Geronimo and the other Apache leaders, including ex-scout Chihuahua, the general stated clearly that if the Apaches surrendered they would be confined in a prison camp in the east, with their families, for not more than two years. At the end of that time they would be brought back to continue their peaceful existence on the reservation at Turkey Creek. General Crook had been authorized by the politicians of Washington to give that promise to the Apaches.

Geronimo trusted General Crook and Britton

1885-1889
President
Grover
Cleveland

Davis probably more than he trusted any other Americans he knew. But politicians he trusted not at all. They had broken their promises too often. Their conduct over the pledged reservation at Warm Springs was merely a typical example of their treacherous tongues.

Still, the return march into American territory began. The regular soldiers went first with their baggage and supplies. Next came the Indian scouts with their red headbands and rifles. Finally came the fiercely independent Apaches of Geronimo. They knew vaguely that they were to be sent by rail to a far-off country called Florida, and the thought of being shipped out like cattle from their native territory insulted them more and more as they approached the end of their journey.

The party camped that night near San Bernardino Springs on the border. An American trader named Tribolet supplied both troops and Indians with mescal. Perhaps something in Tribolet's attitude, possibly something he may have said, reawakened the Apaches' suspicions. They began to suspect they were being led into some kind of trap.

That night some of those Apaches made a last pathetic escape. While the camp was asleep, twenty men, thirteen women, three boys, and three girls slipped away in the darkness. The leader of the group was Geronimo, and along with him were Naiche, Lozen, the splendid woman warrior, and the aged Nana.

This break marked the end of General Crook's efforts to obtain peace and justice for the Apaches. He was replaced immediately by General Nelson A. Miles.

Miles was a less humane officer than his predecessor. Under his harsh orders, troops garrisoned all water holes and established patrols in the mountain passes equipped with heliostats, or mirrors used for the transmission of messages in Morse code. Nearly all the Indian scouts were dismissed.

General
Nelson A. Miles

The Chiricahua and Bedonkohe Apaches who reached Fort Apache were hurriedly loaded into trains and sent eastward to Fort Marion in Florida. With them also went 75 men and about 325 women and children who had resisted all Geronimo's efforts to make them leave the reservation. In addition, many of the Indian scouts, without whose services the white troops would have been helpless in the past, were sent off with the rest of the prisoners. A number of them, including Chato, were still wear-

ing the medals given them by the United States Army in recognition of their valuable service.

This final act of treachery was too much for Lieutenant Davis. He resigned his commission and went off to manage a cattle ranch in Chihuahua. Years later General Miles wrote a stuffy and pompous autobiography. Davis said of the book:

One hundred pages, about one sixth of the entire book, were given to his efforts to complete the conquest of this remnant of the hostiles with 5000 troops at his command. He must have considered it a feat of no small importance.

The graying old wolf, Geronimo, was now fifty-seven years of age. He knew that no future awaited him and his tiny band of followers. Their future was hopeless; there was nowhere for them to go, nowhere they might find a place to rest. The great

American nation was united in its efforts to capture and condemn this last Indian leader who had dared to offer defiance. Newspapers, proud of their humane and democratic views, described Geronimo as a "drunken and dangerous savage . . . an untrustworthy liar . . . a murderer who should be hanged."

Geronimo and his handful of survivors held out for eight months. They were contacted finally by Lieutenant Gatewood, an honorable young officer whom the Apaches liked. The date was August, 1886, the place a forest grove near Sonora's Bavispe River, fifty miles south of the border.

In his book, *The Truth about Geronimo,* Britton Davis quotes his friend, Lieutenant Charles Gatewood, as having officially described the surrender of the Apaches in the following words:

The hostiles came in, unsaddled, and turned out their ponies to graze. Among the last to arrive was Geronimo. He laid down his rifle twenty feet away and came and shook hands. He remarked on my apparent bad health (it was malaria) and asked what was the matter. He took a seat alongside as near as he could get,

Geronimo surrenders

the others in a semicircle, and announced that the whole party was there to listen to General Miles's message.

It took but a minute to say "surrender and you will be sent with your families to Florida, there to await the decision of the President. Accept these terms or fight to the bitter end."

A silence of weeks seemed to fall on the party. They sat with never a movement, regarding me intently. Finally Geronimo passed a hand across his eyes, his hands trembled, and he asked for a drink.

Geronimo's angry first reply was brief. "Take us back to the reservation at Turkey Creek or fight." Then slowly he turned his head to regard his little band of followers: threadbare, lean with hunger, and with little except the rifles they had placed on the ground.

Geronimo gave a despairing shrug and turned to

face Gatewood again. "We want your advice. Consider yourself not a white man but one of us. What should we do?"

Gatewood replied, "Trust General Miles and surrender to him."

The two parties met again the following morning.

"We have decided," said Geronimo. "We are willing to surrender."

Geronimo and his band of Chiricahua were escorted to Fort Bowie. There the statement was again confirmed to them that they would be located with their families at Fort Marion in Florida. They were loaded into boxcars at Holbrook, Arizona, and sent east. But the White Eyes still had one last despicable trick left to play. One can only hope it may have been due to sheer thoughtlessness.

Geronimo's own party was sent to Old Fort Pickens at Pensacola, several hundred miles away from Fort Marion. Among them were Lozen and old Nana. There was no reunion with the members of their families already at Fort Marion for these Indians.

During the year that followed, the Apaches at Fort Marion and those far away at Fort Pickens began to die in alarming numbers. Many of the deaths were due to malaria fever, but others seem to have been caused by grief and a sense of complete hopelessness. In 1887, both groups were sent to the healthier location of Mount Vernon Barracks, Alabama, where they were finally reunited. The change was made as a result of the intercession of President Grover Cleveland and the shocked protests of a number of honorable American individuals, headed by General Crook himself.

Geronimo and his Chiricahua remained in Alabama for six years. By that time old Nana was dead and so was Lozen. In 1894, they were again moved, this time to Fort Sill, Oklahoma. General Miles, however, continued to protest loudly against such improvements being made in the treatment of the Apaches. And so did other citizens.

In 1913, a group of 187 Chiricahua were taken to the Mescalero Apache reservation in New Mexico. (The remaining hundred or so preferred to stay in a state of semi-liberty in the vicinity of Fort Sill.) After twenty-seven years of imprisonment, these Apaches finally returned to their native territory.

Geronimo did not live to see the deserts, the arroyos, and the snow-covered crests of the sierras again. On February 17, 1909, the eighty-year-old warrior, the last war chief of his tribe, reached the end of his defiant career. He died peacefully at dawn, softly chanting "The Morning Song," a hymn to Ussen, the god of the Apache nation. Right to the last, his attitude toward the White Eyes remained what it had been years earlier when he was invited to surrender.

His words then had been:

This is my home. Here I stay. Kill me if you wish, for every living thing has to die sometime. How can a man die better than in fighting for his own?

Geronimo 1829 - 1909

BIBLIOGRAPHY

Ball, Eve, *In the Days of Victorio: Recollections of a Warm Springs Apache.* Tucson, Arizona: University of Arizona Press, 1970.

Barrett, S.M. (ed.) *Geronimo; His Own Story.* New York: Ballantine Books, 1972.

Bourke, John G., *On the Border with Crook.* New York: Charles Scribner's Sons, 1891. Paper edition: Lincoln, Nebraska: University of Nebraska Press, 1971.

Clark, LaVerne Harrell, *They Sang for Horses.* Tucson, Arizona: University of Arizona Press, 1966.

Davis, Britton, *The Truth About Geronimo.* New Haven: Yale University Press, 1963.

Goodwin, Grenville, (edited by Keith H. Basso), *Western Apache Raiding and Warfare.* Tucson, Arizona: University of Arizona Press, 1971.

ABOUT THE AUTHOR

Ronald Syme's early days were spent in an old castle in his native Ireland. Before he was nine he had the free run of the library in his home, thereby acquiring a love of reading. In later boyhood, he spent a few years in New Zealand, mostly hunting wild pig and trout fishing with his sports-loving father. At eighteen he went to sea and visited many parts of the world. About the same time he began writing short stories and feature articles. In 1934 he left the sea to become a journalist. During World War II Mr. Syme first served as ship's gunner, but later transferred to the British Army Intelligence Corps in which he saw service in North Africa and Europe.

Today Ronald Syme, a well-known author in both England and the United States, lives in the peaceful South Pacific island of Rarotonga. His home is a century-old, white-walled stone house within two hundred yards of a beautiful lagoon. The shelves of his library are lined with books, and he can check almost any historical fact he needs for his writing. He enjoys, he says, "most of the advantages of civilization without the corresponding disadvantages."